Items should be returned on or before the last date shown below. Items not already requested by other borrowers may be renewed in person, in writing or by telephone. To renew, please quote the number on the barcode label. To renew online a PIN is required. This can be requested at your local library.
Renew online @ **www.dublincitypubliclibraries.ie**
Fines charged for overdue items will include postage incurred in recovery. Damage to or loss of items will be charged to the borrower.

Leabharlanna Poiblí Chathair Bhaile Átha Cliath
Dublin City Public Libraries

Dublin City
Baile Átha Cliath

Brainse Bhaile Thormod
Ballyfermot Library   Tel. 6269324

Date Due	Date Due	Date Due
07. DEC 11		
23. APR		
28. NOV 12		
2 1 JUL 2014		

"Hari's World presents safety in a way that appeals to children and adults alike and which will reduce accidents in and around water"
The Royal Life Saving Society UK

 Symbols indicate the number of hazards on the page

Hari at the Beach

by Tristan McGee

Edited by Sarah Cheeseman

Illustrated by Pixel Circus

This edition first published 2010 by Hari's World Limited

Copyright © 2010 Hari's World Limited

'Hari' is a registered trademark

A CIP catalogue record of this book is available from the British Library

ISBN 978-0-9559979-6-9

Printed in England

All rights reserved

Mixed Sources
Product group from well-managed forests and other controlled sources
www.fsc.org Cert no. TT-COC-002495
© 1996 Forest Stewardship Council

CarbonNeutral® printing company

Hari at the Beach
Oops Hari!®

Tristan McGee

It was a warm, sunny day at the beach. Hari, Moe and Max were having lots of fun playing in the soft golden sand.

Moe had built some sandcastles and was sitting on top of one of them, quietly humming a tune to himself.

Max was busy digging a hole, making the sand go everywhere.

"Come on," said Hari, "let's go for a swim!"

As an excited Hari turned to pick up his floatation ring, Max spotted Pinch the crab sitting by his little rock pool enjoying the sunshine and minding his own business...

..."Uh-oh! Here we go again!" said Moe.

Pinch leapt into his rock pool and hid in the shadows beneath a large rock.

Hari, Moe and Max peered into the rock pool looking for Pinch.

"*I'll get him out,*" said Hari, poking around in the shallow water with his *favourite stick*.

Hari saw Pinch's claws sticking out and jabbed at them.

"*Don't annoy him, Hari,*" Moe warned, "*he might pinch you!*"

Pinch jumped out of his rock pool and ran off
down the beach towards the old pier.

"*This is great fun!*" barked Max.

Max chased Pinch,
Hari chased Max
and Moe chased Hari.

Pinch ran along the pier as fast as his little legs would carry him...

...his feet clattering on the old wooden boards and his claws clicking loudly above his head.

When Pinch reached the end of the old pier, he jumped off and turned to wave goodbye to Hari, Moe and Max, grinning mischievously.

"Don't go too close to the edge of the pier!" shouted Moe...

...but Hari was running too fast to stop!

Just as Hari was about to follow Pinch off the end of the pier, Max grabbed Hari and Moe grabbed Max. Hari stopped suddenly, and his *favourite stick* flew out of his hand.

Oops Hari!

Pinch landed in the water with a loud...

'SPLASH!'

...Just missing the old shipwreck hidden below the surface. Mrs Peli was sitting on her nest feeling amused.

Back on the beach, Hari and Max dug a deep hole in the sand...

...while Moe decorated his sandcastles with some pretty shells washed up by the waves.

"*Don't dig too deep,*" said Moe...

...but Hari and Max weren't listening, as they were having too much fun.

Suddenly, Pinch ran past them on his way to the cliff, waving Hari's *favourite stick* in the air...

..."*Oh no, not again!*" said Moe.

Hari, Moe and Max began to chase after Pinch towards the cliff
at the other end of the beach.

They clambered over the slippery rocks covered in seaweed and algae,
and ran through the cold spray from the crashing waves.

When Pinch reached the bottom of the cliff, he looked up and saw his friend Peck the seagull asleep in his nest.

Maybe I can escape up there, thought Pinch.

Pinch scrambled up the cliff face towards Peck's ledge.

"We shouldn't climb up there, it looks dangerous," said Moe ... but Hari and Max weren't listening and followed Pinch.

When Hari, Max and Moe reached a narrow ledge, they tried to balance while looking up at Peck and Pinch on the ledge just above them.

Startled by all the noise, Peck woke up and gave a loud

' SQUAWK! '

while Pinch clicked his claws angrily and waved the stick at Hari, Max and Moe.

All this excitement caught Hari and Max by surprise, and they lost their balance and came tumbling down the side of the cliff...

Oops Hari!

...luckily, they landed safely
in a large rock pool
with a big...

'SPLASH!'

Back on the beach, resting in the shade of his umbrella, Hari squirted sun cream everywhere while Moe had a refreshing drink of water.

After all the excitement of chasing Pinch, Max was hungry and searched the large lunchbox for a tasty treat.

Hari and Moe put on their bright red armbands and grabbed their floatation rings, before running down to the water for a swim.

"*Stay close to an adult and make sure the lifeguard can see you,*" warned Moe.

Hari splashed water over Max, who was practising his doggy paddle.

Moe paddled about with his floatation ring, quietly humming a tune and watching Peck circle above them.

What a perfect day this is turning out to be, thought Moe.

Back at his rock pool, Pinch came up with a plan!

He gathered his friends together so they could help him put the plan into action.

Pinch led his friends along the sea bed until they could see Hari, Moe and Max above them.

Very quietly, they swam up through the clear blue water and each chose a bottom to pinch!

Max let out a loud...

' **YELP!** '

...as he ran from the water
with a crab attached to
his bottom!

Oops Hari!

Hari followed Max, and Moe followed Hari...

...chased across the sand by Pinch and his friends.

Peck thought this was great fun, and he flew about, squawking loudly.

Worn out and safely back under their umbrella, Hari, Moe and Max enjoyed an ice cream together and talked about their eventful day at the beach.

"I hope that's the last we see of Pinch today," said Moe.

But Max had other ideas!

There are three books currently available
in the Oops Hari! series for you to enjoy

When Hari gets up late from his nap, he has to rush to meet his friends,
but he can't find his bicycle helmet. Moe is trying to tell him
where it is, but Hari just isn't listening!

ISBN 978-0-9559979-0-7

When Sting the wasp flies into Hari's bedroom on a lazy Saturday morning,
Max the dog begins a chase that leads them all over the house
and garden. Moe tries to warn Max about annoying Sting,
but Max just isn't listening!

ISBN 978-0-9559979-4-5

When Pinch the crab is found in his little rock pool on a sunny day
at the beach, Hari and Max the dog begin a chase that leads
them along the beach and the pier to the cliff bottom.
Moe tries to warn them about annoying Pinch,
but they just aren't listening. When Hari
and his friends go for a swim,
Pinch has other ideas!

ISBN 978-0-9559979-6-9